RNR

SOME ONE
SWEET
ANGEL CHILE

By Sherley Anne Williams

Poetry

SOME ONE SWEET ANGEL CHILE

THE PEACOCK POEMS

Nonfiction

GIVE BIRTH TO BRIGHTNESS

Sherley Anne Williams

SOME ONE
SWEET
ANGEL CHILE

WILLIAM MORROW AND COMPANY, INC.

New York   *1982*

Library of Congress Catalog Card No.: 81-18752

ISBN: 0-688-01012-1
ISBN: 0-688-01177-2 (pbk)

Printed in the United States of America

First Edition

1 2 3 4 5 6 7 8 9 10

BOOK DESIGN BY MICHAEL MAUCERI

In memory of my mother, Lena-Lelia Marie,
and her brother, John Wesley Siler,

for their only surviving brother,
James Lee Robinson

they love the land and did stay

CONTENTS

LETTERS FROM A
NEW ENGLAND NEGRO

REGULAR REEFER

THE SONGS OF THE GROWN

WITNESS   69

LETTERS FROM
A NEW ENGLAND NEGRO

. . . and every member rejoiced
in a single segment made whole
with the circle
in the recognition
of a single voice . . .

Mrs. Josiah Harris
No. 5 The Grange Street
Newport, Rhode Island

August 25, 1867

Dear Miss Nettie,

The School is in a spinney
down behind the old Quarters
where many of the freedmen
live. The teachers, myself
included, live in the Big
House, which—thus far!—has stirred
little comment among the
local whites.

The School is the largest
public building in which blacks
and whites can safely congregate.
Sunday services are held there
and many of the freedmen
attend. Miss Esther introduced
me to several as "the
herald of Emancipation's
new day."

They murmured discreetly
among themselves, the women
smiling quickly, the men
nodding or cutting their
eyes toward me. Finally an
older man stepped forward, "I'm is
Peter, Miss Patient Herald,"
he said, pumping my hand. Then,
with great satisfaction,
"Lotsa room in the Big House.

                              Now."

Mr. Edward Harris
5 The Grange Street
Newport, Rhode Island

August 25, 1867

Edward, I do know <u>some</u> of
whom they speak, especially
the ones now dead, Pope and Homer,
though I cannot read the Greek;
such discussions are the dreams
I dreamed myself in that one
short year at school. But Homer,
as you warned, does not so often
figure in conversation
as I had supposed.

I nod
and smile as Miss Nettie bade
me, but my silence is more
noticeable here than at
her table. I have told my
tale of meeting Emerson
while a servant for the Straights;
they have marveled at that lucky
fate. And only after the
moment passes do I
remember the humorous
exchange between some children
or my comical fright at
walking through the spinney.

2

We sit on the veranda
most evenings and sometimes Beryl
consents to play for us. The
Old Nights gather then in this
southern dusk: Mistress at the
piano, light from twin
candelabra bringing
color to her cheeks, French doors
open to the darkness;
listeners sitting quietly
in the heat.

Now and then
beneath the country airs that
are Beryl's specialty comes a
snatch of melody such as
no mistress ever played and
I am recalled to the present
place. Freedmen sing here now. It
is Cassie or Miss Esther who
turns the music's page. Or myself.

Miss Ann Spencer
Lyme on Eaton
New Strowbridge, Connecticut

August 30, 1867

Dear Ann,

Caution is not so necessary
here as in some other parts
of the state, but we hear of
the "night-riding" and terror
and so are careful. Yet, Miss
Esther's bearing is such that
she is accorded grudging
civility by even
rabid Rebels and though there
was at first some muttering
at young white women teaching
"nigras," Cassie and Beryl are
likewise accepted; thus the
School escapes reprisals.

And,
if the local ladies lift
their skirts aside as I pass—
Well, perhaps I <u>should</u> smirch them.

If my cast-off clothes are
thought unsuited to my station,
my head held too high as I
step back to let the meanest white
go before me, why— What then
is a concert in Newport
or a day in Boston compared
to the chance to be arrogant
amongst so many southerners!

Dear Edward,

The children, I am told, had
little notion of order
and none of school. The first months
here, by all accounts, were
hectic. New students came daily
and changed their names almost
as often, or came and went
at will and those that stayed, talked
throughout the lesson.

They sit
now as prim as Topsy must
have done when first confronted
with Miss Ophelia, hands
folded neatly, faces lit
with pious expectancy.
We teach them to read and write
their names, some basic sums and
talk to them of Douglass and
Tubman and other heroes
of the race.

They are bright
enough—as quick as any
I taught in Newport. Yet behind
their solemn stares, I sense a
game such as I played with those
mistresses who tried to teach
me how best to do the very
task for which I had been
especially recommended,
and so suspect that what we
call learning is in them mere
obedience to some rules.

October 22, 1867

The girls are bold, fingering
our dresses, marveling at
our speech. They cluster around
us at recess, peppering
us with questions about the
North and ourselves. Today, one
asked why I did not cover
my head or at least braid my
hair as is decent around
white folk. We do not speak of
hair in the north, at least in
public, and I answered sharply,
It is not the custom in
the North and I am from the
North—meaning, of course, that I
am freeborn.

I know how
chancy freedom is among
us and so have never
boasted of my birth. And
they were as much stung by my
retort as I by their question.
But in the moment of my
answer the scarves worn by the
women seemed so much a symbol
of our slavery that I would
have died before admitting
my childhood's longing for just
such patient plaiting of my
tangled hair or cover now
my wild and sullen head.

November 10, 1867

Dear Miss Nettie,

My group numbers twenty, aged
four through sixteen, now that
harvest is done. There are no
grades, of course, and Tuesday
nights I take a group of grown-ups
over the lessons I give the
youngsters the following week.

The
grown-ups are more shy with me
than with Miss Esther and the
others, seldom speaking unless
I have done so first and then
without elaboration.

I did not expect immediate
kinship as Beryl chides: I am
as stiff with them as they with
me; yet, in unguarded moments,
I speak as they do, softly
a little down in the throat
muting the harsh gutterals and
strident diphthongs on my tongue.

November 24, 1867

There was in Warwick Neck, at
the time we lived there, a black
woman called Miss Girt whose aunt
had bought her out of slavery
in the District some fifty
years before. She was a
familiar and striking figure
in that town where there were few
negroes; of that color we
called smoothblack—a dense and
even tone that seems to drink
the light. The strawberry pink
of her mouth spilled over onto
the darkness of her lips and
a sliver of it seemed to
cut the bottom one in two.

She kept a boarding house for
negroes, mostly men who worked
at odd jobs up and down the
Coast. The white children whispered
about it—though the house
differed only in being
set in a larger plot with
two or three vacant ones between
it and its nearest neighbors.
It was the closest thing to
a haunted house the town provided
and on idle afternoons
the white children "dared

the boogey man"—though they seldom
got close enough to disturb
Miss Girt or her boarders with
their rude calls and flourishes—
and withdrew giggling and
pushing at the slightest
movement or noise.

We went also,
on our infrequent trips
to town, to see the boogey
man and sometimes heard a strain
of music, a sudden snatch
of laughter. Or watched the white
children from a distance. Once
George Adam called out, "Here She
come," sending them into clumsy
flight and us into delighted
laughter. Once Miss Girt herself
came round the corner on the
heels of their cry, "Nigger!"

"And
a free one, too," she called and
laughed at their startled silence.
They fled in disorder,
routed, so George said, by the
boldness of this sally, and,
I thought, by the hot pink in
the laughing dark of Miss Girt's face.

Edward dearest,

They persist in calling me
Patient though I have tried to
make it clear that neither
Emancipation nor Patience
is part of my given name.
They understand the Herald
part and laugh at Peter who
says he could not then understand
that New England talk. The
following week, I am again
Miss Patient Hannah. I tell
myself, it is not so important
and truly have ceased to argue,
have come indeed to still any
impulse to retort almost
as it is born.

Tonight my
old devil tongue slipped from
me after weeks of careful
holding. I answered roughly
some harmless question, My name
is Hannah. Hannah. There is
no Patience to it.

"Hannah
our name for the sun," Stokes said
in the silence that followed
my remark. "You warm us like
she do, but you more patient
wid us when we come to learn."

December 27, 1867

The men play their bodies like
drums, their mouths and noses like
wind instruments, creating
syncopated rhythms, wild
melodies that move the people
to wordless cries as they dance.
There are true musicians—Givens
who plays the banjo, Lloyd the
fiddler, many singers. Even
the tamborinists and those
who shake the bones coax beauty
from nothingness and desire.
Yet it is the music of
those who play themselves, that tone
half voice, half instrument that
echoes in my head. Tonight at
Stokes' wedding I was moved by
this to moan and dance myself.

My dear,

Beryl sees the poverty of my
childhood as a dim reflection
of the slavery in which
Pansy lived, sees in her, as
indeed in all, some vestige
of my former self that teaching
frees me of.

I see in her,
too, some other Pansy, some
Other, not my self and not
so simple as we thought her.

We have come among Christians
for whom Dance is the crossing
of the feet; what they do not
know of the world is learnable.
It is this I have come to
teach. Beryl has no eye for such
distinctions, seeing only
frenzy where I have been taught
the speech of walk and shout.

Dear Miss Nettie,

The school stands now where the praise
grove was; the grass then was worn
away by bended knees, the
dirt packed hard by shouting feet.

"Go wid Massa, Lawd; go wid
Massa."

Pansy mimics the
old prayer, torso going
in one direction, limbs in
some other. There is laughter,
murmurs of "Do, Lawd" and "Amen."
But it is memory she
dances; the praise grove was gone
before the War, closed by the
Masters' fears.

"Dey ain trus mo'n
one darky alone wid Chris;
two darkies togetha need
a live white man near."

Pansy's
mother and many others
gathered then in twos and threes
in secret clearings in the
woods, quiet witness that
our Savior lives.

"Go wid
Massa, Jesus. Go wid dis
white man.

"And Mista Lincoln
                    did."

Their triumph is renewed
in our laughter, yet there are
some—Pansy I think is one—
who scoff at white men's ways and
gather now in the same hushed
harbors to worship and to
whisper of the new jesus
in the old praise grove's heart.

January 21, 1868

She comes grudgingly
to know the world
within the printed
page yet rejoices
in Stokes' progress

She trusts the power
of the word only
as speech and sets me
riddles whose answers
I cannot speak

How
do the white man school
you
Give a nigga
a hoe

How do he
control you
Put a
mark on some paper
turn our chi'ren to

noughts
How do master
tell darkies apart
By looking at the
lines and dots

I tell
myself it is the
catechism of
unlettered negroes
that one dance has made

me Darky; pagan
and half wild.
She is
as black and lovely
as her namesake's heart

and teases me about
my "learnin"
She would
row my head with seed
plaits And prays I have
not been ruined by

this white man's schooling.

Edward,

I may attend prayer meetings
in the Quarters, go now
and then to the services "Singing"
Johnson leads. If such as
Sister Jones or Mrs. Casper from
the town ask, I may go to
gatherings in their homes. And
I am free to go wherever
Cassie and Beryl are invited.
Thus my need for company
is understood and addressed;
so, I am not to go to
play parties in the Quarters
nor go there of an evening
to Stokes' and Pansy's to talk
and listen at the music and
the tales. Miss Esther is shocked
that I would even consider
such actions without seeking
advice from Beryl or Cassie
or go without asking leave
of herself. It is a stalemate:
she will not give her permission;
I go and ask no one's consent.

I know you are not wholly
knowledgeable of all I
write you, dearest Ann, yet your
own eccentricity at
times allows you to apprehend
what most would miss. And I do
not expect answers or advice.
We stand outside each other's
lives and are enchanted with this
unlikely meeting: the blue-
stockinged white lady, the smart
colored girl. I stand now
outside the life I know as
negro. Sometimes, as I try
to make sensible all that
I would tell you, I see my
self as no more than a
recorder and you a listening
ear in some future house.

Dearest One,

I have no clear recall of
how I came to be at the
door of my first mistress, kept
little of that beginning, save
that through bargaining I fixed
my wage and worked extra for
room and board. I cannot now
remember all the helping
hands I passed through before the
Harrises took me in. There are
things I tell no one and have
ceased to tell myself. I have
grown to womanhood with my past
almost a blank.

I do not
recall, yet the memory
colors all that I am. I
know only that I was a
servant; now my labor is
returned to me and all my
waiting is upon myself.

LITTLE EVA'S TEMPTATION

in bold red print a
girl child emblazoned
below this in a
tattered orange dress
deep brown skin gleaming
against a blue back-
ground vibrant across
all these years:

"Topsy"

As real as when Ms
Stowe first dreamed her, thin
shouldered, bug eyed
beribboned plaits—Arm
and leg raised in some
disjointed prance. Miss
Eva's Temptation:

The knowing grin that
mocks the strings, the
supple body that
mocks the string master's
                dance.

REGULAR REEFER

no No .

     Bessie
        didn't

smoke

   pot Not

   Bessie

nothing like that —

   just

REGULAR REEFER.

        — ruby walker —

for Carlos and Iris Blanco

39. Bessie on my wall: the thick triangular
                            nose wedged
                            in the deep brown
                            face nostrils
                            flared on a last
                            long hummmmmmmmm.

                            Bessie singing
                            just behind the beat
                            that sweet sweet
                            voice throwing
                            its light on me

fifteen: I looked in her face
and seed the woman
I'd become. A big
boned face already
lined and the first line
in her fo'head was
black and the next line
was sex cept I didn't
know to call it that
then and the brackets
round her mouth stood fo
the chi'ren she teared
from out her womb. And
yo name Bessie; huh.
she say. (Every one
call her Ma o' Ol
Lady) Bessie. well.
Le'me hear you sang.
She was looking in
my mouth and I knowed
no matter what words
come to my mind the
song'd be her'n jes as
well as it be mine.

port arthur:

what he do you
nonya

(I seed the eye swolled shut)

how much he take
nonya

(I seed this in a dream)

Make yo hand in a fis'

They jes lay there open
in her lap short stump-
like fingers curved ova
the callused grey-white palms

his ass go when Time come

gir'—she can't talk plain 'count
of her lip—gir' I whip
any bitch that got two
legs won' think twice on it

Make yo hand in a fis'

She ain't heard and her hands
is meaty, deep veined wid
red brown lines a little
lighter than her skin her
nails bite down past the quick

Don' no man jes beat on
me but time I whip my
nigga ass don' care who
right who wrong that's the time
he stop bein my man

what he do you
nonya

(the lower lip puffed and black)

how much he take
nonya

(I seed this in a dream)

Rome Georgia: Dear Sister, enclose
is money as promised.
Sorry it is not as
much as you ast but
the job with the Miller
troop didn't work as ex-
pect. Mr. Miller
run a brownskin show
and say I am black
which they know when
they hire me as I
don try to hide it
(smile) I will con-
tinue on with Ma and
them We play the "81"
in Atlanta which
everyone say is
real nice I send you
more then. Brother Clare
send love.

Your loving
sister,

Bessie

the blues ain't nothin
　　but some man on yo mind
　　　Blues ain't nothin
　　　　but some man on yo mind
　　　　　The one that you lovin
　　　　　　seein some other woman on yo time.

　　them ol young woman Blues

The man that I marry ain't been born
　　his mamma, yo'all, is dead
The man that I marry ain't been born
　　and, girls, you know his mamma is a long time dead.
If Love ain't where I'm at
　　I can always get some on up ahead.

I ain't no high yella
　　I'm a deep killa brown
I ain't no high yella
　　I'm a deep killa brown
Tip yo hat as you enter, Daddy,
　　and again as you go down.

You can call me a hussy
　　cause I likes the road
Call me a hussy
　　but I'mo keep on travelin this road
I'm a good woman and
　　I can get a good man any place I goes.

                    from a
                 picture
              taken at the
              start of her
                     career

the pearls caught
just so in
long fingered
hands and the
hands held close
to the breast

the strength to
break the strand
a smile to
break the heart

and the lines
that bracket
the long lip's
end.
        this is
no yearbook
pose.
        her pearls
were the last
jewels she sold.

Soliloquy from the Trolley Line Home

after a visit to jack:

Pickin my way through
ice and dog shit same
as I did as a
girl, goin to see
this nigga in the
hospital jes like
I did my first
husband, Earl

*Get a
work-in man When you
marry!*
      Ma was hard
on that boy And Love

died. My feet don't
feel no difference
between Tennessee
dirt and these Philly
streets Hurtful as they
is, these is *shoes*, not
somma Clary's out-
groweds and I can reel.
And rock too—

Ma jes
let them songs sing her
like they was the ones
makin the livin
off her—
        Believe that's
what I'll tell these young

womens: Honey, don't
let yo *song* curb you.

. . . a rowboat out on the stormy seas . . .

I was walkin mens when I met you,
honey; it ain't no harm in that.
It wouldn't be blues if I didn't trance
mens to my side. Ma showed me that.

She can walk a man around a tent—
even the ones think they so cute.
This nigga bragged he didn't deal in coal.
I taught him degrees, baby; that's the truth.

Them yellow bitches in the chorus got something
to laugh at now that don't mean me no harm.
Ah, baby—Jack—that walk is a mark
in the family; it's got to be carried on.

the hard time Blues

It wa'n't all moanin and cut'in the fool

This is what you get for sparkle and shine
This what you get for sparkle and shine
A two bit husband and a bitch ain worth a dime

He baked her biscuts, baked em soft and brown
Baked her biscuts, baked em in my bed
While I was out singing in the town

spoken: I could not co-operate with this "Love" plan

Well. The rising sun
    ain't gon set in the East no mo
repeat: I say, the rising sun
      ain't gon set in the East no mo
You done messed around
    and let yo good woman go!

The Empress Brand Trim

ruby reminisces:

He was still Uncle
Jack to me the first
time they come to New
York and I knew she
was special cause he
didn't run his women
in front of us kids.
She rehearsed that first
record right there in
our parlor and I
stayed out of school to
watch her. I didn't know
it then but my whole
life changed. She didn't look
no older than me—
bigger and darker,
sure, but no older,
and I was a teen-
ager—a pretty
girl; I sang; I danced.

She carried herself
like she didn't know she
was ugly, almost
like she didn't know she
was black—buying dark
glasses in Chicago
cause fans recognized

her in the streets or
that night in Concord—
she chased the *Klan* out
from behind our tent;
said she hadn't never
heard of such shit.

She loved womens and
mens. The womens was
on the Q.T., of
course, cause Jack wouldn't play
that. But wasn't nothing
he could do about
the mens. She'd go to
a party and pick out the
finest brown. "I'mo
give *you* some Empress
Brand trim. Tonight you
pay homage to the
Pussy Blues made."
And they always did.

the mule and the world

"Honey, the nigger woman is the mule of the world."

Zora Neale Hurston

Tell my mule, say, tell my mule now,
She sho ain't gots no easy gait.

She done hauled so many ashes
They embedded in that ol rough ass hide.

Them bones knock up against my bones
And they sink all down in my flesh.

This how that Mule respond:

Tell my boss, say, tell my boss, yo'all,
More than him have spread they legs for me.

Walkers ain't got no ride to speak of
But that ain't the mules blues

And this ol girl jes don't want to hear it.

I Want Aretha to Set
This to Music:

I surprise girlhood
in your face; I know
my own, have been a
prisoner of my own
dark skin and fleshy
lips, walked that same high
butty strut despite
all this; rejected
the mask my mother
wore so stolidly
through womanhood and
wear it now myself.

I see the mask, sense
the girl and the woman
you became, wonder
if mask and woman
are one, if pain is
the sum of all your
knowing, victim the
only game you learned.

Old and in pain and
bearing up bearing up
and hurt and age These
are the signs of our
womanhood but I'll
make book Bessie did
more than just endure.

9:

hear it?

/   53

hear it?

Oh I'm lonesome now
    but I won't be lonesome long
Say I'm lonely now
    but I don't need to be lonesome long
You know it take a man wid some style and passion
    to make a single woman sing these lonely songs

    one-sided bed Blues

Never had a man talk to me
    to say the things he say
Never had a man talk like this, honey,
    say the things you say.
Man talk so strong
    till I can't tell Night from Day.

His voice be low words come slow
    and he be movin all the while
His voice be low words come slow
    and he be movin, Lawd! all the while.
I'm his radio and he sho
    know how to tune my dial.

My bed one-sided from me
    sleepin alone all the time
My bed *wop*-sided from me
    sleepin alone so much of the time
And the fact that it empty
    show how this man is messin wid my mind.

𝄢

what's out there knockin
Is what the world
don't get enough of

𝄢

recollections   Man, first time she come to the
studio with Blue—that was
somethin. She was fine as fine
could be. A dark blue suit and
orange feather boa, a
little cloche with a feather
that curved down around her cheek,
all woman—even after she
got heavy, which she wasn't
that day. Blue was tellin folks—
that's *every*one what to do.
I mean, he'd say, Miss Smith—last
time we'd recorded, they'd said
Bessie, not Miss, not Ma'am—don't
like the piano so loud;
Miss Smith want horns right here,
lookin at the arrangements
sayin Mister, sayin please
and steady pickin his teeth.
It was years before I knowed
the man couldn't read no music
that's how strong his talk was.
The white mens didn't know how to
take it. They flash a look at
Bessie and she jes settin
there with them fine legs crossed, one
shoe danglin off the end of
her toe. Aw, man; Bessie was
jes natchally what her
song say: some sweet angel chile.

𝄢

meanin love   meanin love

𝄢

fragments:

Aw just move toward me
baby, like you did
in the woods that day

𝄢:

meanin love

𝄢:

Bessie walk like water yo'all
hold the whole world in her smile
she touched me and I knowed her
saw love as her natchal style

𝄢:

meanin love

𝄢:

O get close to me
honey, be the light
that show me my way

𝄢:

who gon live yo life
till you do? this ain't
Ma I'm talkin to, Let
Blue com-mon in. Let

𝄢:

Ahh come down on me
    baby, see me like
    you saw me that day

Bessie's Blues

I am out of it
And at least I didn't
die But that don't stop
memory which I
know you have some of

too—and if I phoned
it wouldn't be beggin
not even from what
you call a woman
like me Memory

don't have to beg its
own answer but to
call to jes make you
remember what we
won't ever forget

is worse than useless
It hurts us both But
I know how cold it
get when the wind blow
and all you got to

wrap up in is self
and now self have to
stretch and it still don't
fit what it used to
cover So if what you

say you want changes
my side door open
and This really not
beggin Not and what
we have is this good.

The Old Lady Singing of Bessie
(from the portrait finished after her death)

People will tell you a boy is yo heart
and I know you git life wif a girl

A boy may be yo heart
but a woman life tied up in a girl

That's what make you scream make you holla
say, Lawd, it only posed to be one me in this worl'

fragments:

> She was sunlight
> dapplin a man's arm
> the prettiest thing
> I eva seen was
> the color of her
> skin in the light
> comin through them red
> and gold leaves. What
> happen is in the
> record: She could walk
> a man like water;
> she touched me; and I
> knowed her. The rest is
> my own memories.

down torrey pines road:

This could be that road
    in Mississippi
though this one winds up
    the hill from the sea

The way the moonlight washes
    out all colors and
the high beams bounce shadows off
    the overhanging
trees, the way the cars come round the
    curves gathering speed
for the climb up the road to
    the canyon rim is
something like Mississippi
    that stretch of highway
outside Coahoma close by
    Clarksdale and the Jim
Crow ward in the hospital
    that used to be there.

I dare each curve to
    surprise me as I
round it show me the
    rear-end of some truck
before I can stop.

I beep the solitary
    biker, worry that
his leg mounted flash won't shine
    far enough, sweep on
to the traffic light at the
    summit. This is not
the road to Clarksdale. I say
    over and over
what my name is not.

THE SONGS OF THE GROWN

for John Malcolm

their speech was music . . .

WITNESS
for becca

Based on some fleeting
moments of *malletis—*
nigga knowledge
of the white man and
black life—I give voice
to the old stories.
This is not romance,
private fictions spun
from scattered readings
in public documents
bastard logic, nor
Sambo's tricking. This
is a metaphor
liable like Harlem
to be dis/missed in
liberal anthologies
with a changeling
footnote that under
reads the poem Brands
the footnoter Racist.
his every statement
the product of some
evil intent: Witness[1]

[1]a negro section
in the shared past.

Bang! Bang!

beepbeep

beepbeep
ungawa
Black Power

–the provision ground–

for Eleanor and Winnie The Legends of Our Time

The Chem building's down behind Founders
—the library—
in a hollow we call the Valley of Death
On Friday afternoons, the Greek Lines
Rise from the Valley
struttin and chantin
singin stories (to the tune of soul songs
of *Alpha, Kappa* and *Que*

ungawa

The Ad building overlook the GhetTo
that baddd Georgia Avenue where a Block Boy
will Pick a pocket Kick an ass
in a minute
Will do it just on G.P.

They don't like no Frat Walk

Every Friday it's a ritual

the Greek Lines strut
the Block Boys shuck
Some one get down on some body's head.

beepbeep
ungawa

𝄢:

beepbeep
beepbeep

Winter a bitch in D.C.
Trees all over the city
Each one have showered down leaves
Niggas fightin otha niggas—
Lawd. How do people keep
    Livin in this cold

beepbeep

𝄢:

ungawa
beepbeep

The CIA have a Agent on campus
(license number 313

The Summer School Office is bugged

Howard was named for a white man

Freedman's for some unknown black

/   *71*

Yet no body know how it happen:

The Frat boys and the Block Boys
Rose out that Valley, together
burned the effigy of a General
Named Hershey And one of Howard!

ooooowWWW up in *hyeah*

beepbeep

And
No One
Know

How it happen
Whether it was something
to do with the season
With just that Time and that place

but we was tOGathA
takin names behind more than
some jive-time ol Draft.

BLACK POWER
Black Power
black power
black power

ungawa

ungawa

beepbeep

𝄢

She had known brothers

And imagined her
self hip, comparing
her deep tan to
Caro's fair skin
swaggering as she
thought a black dyke would
try'na pass old jokes
off as wit, calling
everyone man

These were passing impressions
they paid her little
attention: the sun
struck no lights in her
straw colored hair like
it lit in Caro's
red naps, Tonia's
top heavy loose-limbed
amble eluded
her; they were rough

Sisters

Warming each
other with memory
and mind And colder
than she thought them
forgiving much
reading ignorance
as often as
arrogance in her
accent, giving warnings
that she took as bluff

She saw in their glow
some remembrance
of browned flesh; the thumb
jerked carelessly in
Caro's face aped old
desires. Caro's flash
almost killed her. Her
time with brothers made
her no place with us.

Big Red and His Brothers

afta its all ova
everyone can say what
shoulda been done. We went
with Red and his brothers—
course, Big Red was Malcolm
by then—and for the first
time we was women to
men in the world. So, when
He died at the hands of
the Police, we waited
for the brothers to step
forward, at least one from
amongst those that had
survived. Well, Red lived as
Malcolm; he died our crown
prince. His brothers turned Black
meat pretty and brought
desire in place of love.

a young woman's blues

I tell a dude in
a minute, better
get your business straight
before coming to
talk that talk to me

cause a cat got to
be together with
his own self before
he try to get it
together with me.

But even with your
stuff this shakey, I'd
want to be forty
if it meant you'd talk
your talk with me.

Ain't
nobody can be
raised twice—and that took
me a while to learn.

I only got one
child, that's my son and
I got enough to
do trying to get
him and me through the

world. But you a man.
And it's been some time
since I thought of my
self as a girl so

forty would be just
another number
if me being how
ever much older
would let you get down

would help us deal in
some, well, righteous love.

32

pretty blue his eyes
his wide lipped mouth put
in this poem and the
curve of my neck a
round the hard bud of
my breast
            the eye with
in his eye (blue large
pupils black my face
mirrored there the light
perhaps a crystal
stone:
            his
mouth full lips wide
lips dark blowing my
ear or lips tight teeth
bared the climax name
less screaming: the ear
to hear hear his lips
dark covering my own.

Straight Talk from Plain Women

Evangeline made her
own self over in
'65, say she
looked in the mirror
at her face saw it
was pretty (her legs
was always fine and
she'd interrupt a
dude's rap to say how
it was a common
characteristic
amongst our women

Did
the same thang with her
neck pointin to
its length, its class. And
we dug where she
was comin from specially
that pretty part, how
she carried herself
with style, said go'n girl
so be it.

Evangeline made her
self over and who
eva else didn't see
We is her witness.

beepbeep

Middle Passage

for Marvin El Muhajir

The land is just names
the bus pass through or
by-pass: Rest Stops, the
waiting rooms dingy
even in newness;
WHITE ONLY signs stare
now from white eyes. One
little backwater
town come after the
other with just this
highway, this greyhound
in between.

Buses
seem to enter through
the back doors of a
city, lumbering
down streets way too small
for them past vacant
buildings and junked cars.
And it always seem
to be dark when the
bus pull into the
station. That station
be the brightest among
all the night lights.

generations

mamma is a
silent movie
daddy a shadow
on the screen I hear
their voice in Honky
Tonk wonder see their
lips move in speechless
quiet on the screen

this is a season
of singing of fall
out and love in West
Texas and California
in a pick-up truck
of the present and
the last crop

my mamma is a movie she shine on
Daddy's screen they framed
now in Arvin a
place where we picked hops
a time up in Hillsborough
and past and present
stop

this is a season
of singing in the
towns and the cities
from coast to coast of
searching in the
wilderness for what
we thought was loss

THE ICONOGRAPHY OF CHILDHOOD

i

A town less
than ten stories tall

Spring rains wash the wind
light annihilates
distance
snow flecked Sierras
loom at land's end

Land flat as hoecake
Summers hot enough
to fry one Crops fanned

out in fields far as
eyes can see
every
Time we work a row
another appears
on the horizon

These are tales told in darkness
in the quiet at the ends
of the day's heat, surprised in
the shadowed rooms of houses
drowsing in the evening sun.

In this one there is music
and three women; some child is
messing with the Victrola.
Before Miss Irma can speak
Ray Charles does of "The Nightime"
and *Awww* it Is the fabled

music *yo'alls* seldom given
air play in those Valley towns
heard mostly in the juke-joints
we'd been toold About; and so
longed for in those first years in
the Valley it had come to

seem almost illicit to
us. But the women pay us
no mind. We settle in the
wonder of the music and
their softly lit faces listening
at the songs of our grown.

iii

Summer mornings we
rose early to go
and rob the trees
bringing home the
blossoms we were told
were like a white girl's
skin And we believed
this as though we'd
never seen a white
girl except in
movies and magazines.

We handled the
flowers roughly
sticking them in oily
braids or behind
dirty ears laughing
as we preened ourselves;
savoring the brown
of the magnolias'
aging as though our color
had rubbed off
on the petals' creamy
flesh transforming some
white girl's face into
ornaments for our
rough unruly heads.

iv

We never knew the
woman her brothers
later told us was
Lena though we could
see that mamma was
a shadow of some
former self, her down
home ways worn down to
nubs.

They laid this on
"yo'daddy," the way
he'd changed her name
because Lena didn't
suit him. Well, "Lelia"
never seemed right to
them bowing and
scraping (as they phrased
it) before "yo'-
daddy"—after the
way she'd fought *mens* as
a girl.

Daddy blamed
it on her own
foolishness from which
even he couldn't save
her—that Siler blood
he told us; he had
rescued her, brought her

out of Texas. And
she'd have already
what her brothers wrote
home about; if it
wasn't for her own
ol country ways.

v

The buildings of the
Projects were arrayed
like barracks in
uniform rows we
called regulation
ugly, the World in
less than one square block.
What dreams our people
had dreamed there seemed to
us just like the Valley
so much heat and dust.

Home training was
measured by the day's
light in scolds and
ironing cords; we
slipped away from chores
and errands from
orders to stay in
call to tarry in
the streets: gon learn what
downhome didn't teach.

And
Sundown didn't hold us
long. Yet even then
some grown-up sat still
and shadowed waiting
for us as the sky
above the Valley
                    dimmed.

vi

Showfare cost a lot
but we ran the
movies every chance
we got, mostly grade
B musicals that
became the language
of our dreams.   Baby
Lois sang in the
rain for the hell of
it; Helen was a
vamp.   Ruise was the
blood-red rose of
Texas, her skin as
smooth and dark as a
bud with just a hint
of red.

Sweating and
slightly shamefaced, we
danced our own routines
seeing our futures
in gestures from some
half remembered films.
We danced crystal
sidewalks thrilled in the
arms of neighborhood
boys and beheld our
selves as we could be
beyond the Projects:
the nine and ten year
old stars of stage and
screen and black men's hearts.

vii

My mother knew what
figure she cut in
the world and carried
that hurt in silence,
once in great whiles roused
by some taunt or threat
to rage mutely then
settling back to
mutter angrily
and to sleep.   By the
time I come to my
first memory of
her face she was
already mamma
as I knew her for
the rest of her life.
I saw a ghost in
flashes in lumbering
fury and shaking
laughter glowing
pretty.   In these
remembered glimpses
I know the woman
Lena who was sister
to my uncles John
and Jimmy who
married Jesse Winson
and died on the
Texas Panhandle
years before my birth:
taciturn, quick
tempered, *hell-thay*,
my uncles said.

the wishon line

i

The end of a line
is movement the
process of getting
on, getting off, of
moving right along

The dank corridors
of the hospital
swallowed him up
(moving right along
now—from distant
sanatorium
to local health care
unit—the end of
that line is song:
*T.B. is killing
me* We traveled some
to see Daddy on
that old Wishon route
but the dusty grave
swallowed him up.

ii

These
are the buses of
the century running
through the old wealth of
the town, Huntington
Park, Van Ness Extension
the way stops of
servants; rest after
miles of walking and
working: cotton, working
grapes, working hay. The
end of this line is
the County: County
Hospital, County
Welfare.   County Home—
(moving right on—No
one died of T.B.
in the 50's; no one
rides that Line for free.

The Green-Eyed Monsters of the Valley Dusk

sunset knocks the edge from the
day's heat, filling the Valley
with shadows: Time for coming
in getting on; lapping fields
lapping orchards like greyhounds
racing darkness to mountain
rims, land's last meeting with still
lighted sky.

This is a car
I watched in childhood, streaking
the straightaway through the dusk
I look for the ghost of that
girl in the mid-summer fields
whipping past but what ghosts lurk
in this silence are feelings
not spirit not sounds.

Bulbous
lights approach in the gloom
hovering briefly between
memory and fear, dissolve
into fog lamps mounted high
on the ungainly bodies
of reaping machines: Time
coming in. Time getting on.

california light

1.   North County

The freeway is a river
of light rounding the base of
Mt. Soledad, its distant
drone a part of the night. I've
watched in the darkness as the
river dimmed to the fitful
passing of solitary
cars and heard the coyotes
in the canyon crying their
survival to the strange land

I booted up one day, walked
out across the mesa that
fronts along my place till the
land was a shallow cup around
me and the houses were lost
in the distance on its
rim. The plants were the only
life I saw—muted greens dry
browns bursts of loud purple and
lighter blues, brilliant in the
spring light; something rustled the
undergrowth; a jet murmured
in the softly clabbered sky.

The Indian dead are here
buried beneath Spanish place
names and the cities of the
pioneers and the droning
silence is witness to what
each has claimed, what each owned.
My father's grave is here some
where his tale lost like that jet
in clabber his children
scattered along the river
voices singing to the night.

2.   miss le'a's chile

I

I have come in my own time
to the age at which she bore
me, rooted among memories
made phantom by my thoughts
say . . . She was a weaver, born
in an age of ready-made
cloth studying over threads
and colors while some machine
stamped her man's health, Nourishment
for the Kids, the dreams of her
youth, Two Bedrooms in the Project—
But these are symbols of
memory, not memories
themselves, the meat of vision
unfolding. The past does not
always come when you call it.

II

We are there, herded through the
hard clear light, but I do not
see us crossing the graveled
lot, only the shadows of
the cream-colored houses and
white men in brown suits as one
is jerked to the ground. I know
that ball of flesh and dress is
mamma, her roar precedes her

and this the time the County
declared her "unfit" and called
in the sheriff. This is a
symbol of Project-County;
the face of the woman who
fought so is memoried in the
flesh of Miss Lelia's daughters.

the earth woman

I am always rushed
into their living
rooms; I lie upon
my back This is what
I came for what I
know of love strange
ceilings my own
heavy breathing a
match flaring briefly;
some wayward whisper
sounding in this act.
I could talk that talk
if they would listen—
I am not an orphan

But these men don't care
a thing about me
Or if they do it's
some paradise behind
my eyes that my body
might be key to

They
look up in wonder
from enjoyment of
my cock It is not
what they came to me
for, This eden: too
much and not enough

I believe I am
made to be a full
                    cup

d.c. visions: the verified tongue

*for sterling: you know
you was my dream*

My
tongue break like water
the breeze turn me all
around. The streets come
down so heavy my
mind don't know what all
my eyes have seen, who
known me; who wo'e my
name. This land rode me
that road lead me here.

And you some dream I
didn't even know I
was dreaming. In your
face I trace my father's
I listen at my
mother's voice. And each
time like the first time
I come to that house
Miss Daisy meet me
at the gate she have
my sister's walk.

The
bridge over P Street;
that ol half-assed hill;
the Valley up at
Howard. My heart do
live in the stillness
of the city. This
city hold me in
silence each separate
sound be some song and
I tremble and moan
in this warm darkness
I tremble and moan
at such peace.

The Janus Love

𝄢:

The simple
extravagances
of speech that carry
loving
      As fleeting
as a moment
        the
twoness of this
single touch
          if one
had surfeit
        if *feel*
were all and not
enough
After
laughing after love
in touch I have
surprised song in your
throat: terror touches
me I am panicked
by my own flesh.

9:

I have driven through
darkness and crouch in
my son's lighted room
carry-on with his
covers gently rock
his bed The noise I
hear is you as you
enter rubbing your
eyes half nude The strong
feet and stronger thighs
the arms and lightly
muscled chest are what
I fled and the self
I could not look at
through your eyes and I'm
tired And drugged with speed
with recent grief but
oh you gather me
in so much sunshine
rey in goodness and
I'm gathered baby
gathered gathered in

I'm prim proper that
and some others are
faces used so long
I forget that say
I have legs or talk
a different tongue that
the masks are part self
not myself's total.
I have no other
way to face the world
except this secret
changing of my face
that your surprise in
silence show me with
quiet care so I
am bare in your sight
and bear your knowing.

I see your sum through
your silence see now
my old fear through your
eyes your quickness slowed
by how I face the
world Me stripped by love
of all the needed
masks driven into
a closet but most
of all your quickness
slowed as it is slowed
now by your fear Oh
I am prim even
Proper but I cross
my legs with you.

I would deny all
previous knowledge
start us over And
this time would not end
with a pat on the
booty a pretense
that the common
rhetoric of scores
and read-me is our
creole for concern.

This time
I would be honest
not
    -some-woman-out
    -to-cop-some-
                brotha
I am that lady
you own self's drumming
you the singer in
my flesh

Let the future
shape this coming I
would surrender to

        its strumming

wrapped in gold against
the window light love
lies like a tawny
cat sunning on the
vermilion carpet

I nibble the thick
lobe, tongue the tightly
furled gristle of an
ear Lap the sleek bronze
head between my thighs
The butterfly mouth drips
honey
    The muscle
grown long and chunky
lapped by hand by mouth
its length fed and slaked
now in body's bed

I am suckled on
this flat breast

nightbird

I have not cried my
last at Vangy's death
learned what parts of her
her going left have
not asked to look in
to the future to
see how my boy and
I recover or
if and cannot say
with whom but I head
for the place you said
you'd be not caring
about the threat of
cold rain of being
gathered in knowing
only that if you
enter you enter
by the key I gave.

a record for my friends

1

It was a season
when even music
was expensive; dimes
pennies even nickels
appeared beside turn
tables
       We learned the
price of old favorites
and paid it, citing
Allen each time we
dropped that dime—College
brotha knoow the
value of records
had a stereo
And a collection

He had risen above this.

once in a moment
of passion paying
$.35 to
       steady the tone-arm
so Watson & Duke
could blow the stomp down
Blues listening like
every revolution
of the record was
his own

       his love was
our cloak and our crown.

2

i

War is Eldridge's next
reincarnation
laid back and funky
turned dippty dip and
one note

"Why can't we be friends?"
and Mao in the
moon: the sheik of freak
on jesus this is
the last cliché They
have snickered at
Fidel and he out
lived them.

ii

We flicker
the same way we flame
briefly *"real is real"*
One always do know;

All they say about
California is
true.

coda

I have come to
hear Monk
forever funky
and laid glowing Growing
solo and gold giving
birth to no one
so much as himself.

3

I have lived without
music except what
I could play in my
head—O radio
defended me, the
Happy Harolds of
the ghetto, souling
in a grubby war
with silence and sales
the mean substitute
for song

It's about
someone saying what
the next theme will be
and spe*ech R*each.
                              for
it
And we do. driven
on gypsy chords to
root the word now
fluid
            well
No.   the mind
is not music Get

what you love by heart
Play this for your friends.

you were never miss brown to me

I

We were not raised to look in
a grown person's mouth when they
spoke or to say ma'am or sir—
only the last was sometimes
thought fast even rude but daddy
dismissed this: it was yea and
nay in the Bible and this
was a New Day.   He liked even
less honorary forms—Uncle,
Aunt, Big Mamma—mamma to
who? he would ask.   Grown
people were Mr. and Miss
admitting one child in many
to the privilege of their
given names.   We were raised to
make "Miss Daisy" an emblem
of kinship and of love; you
were never Miss Brown to me.

II

I call you Miss in tribute
to the women of that time,
the mothers of friends, the friends
of my mother, mamma
herself, women of mystery
and wonder who traveled some
to get to that Project.   In the
places of their childhoods, the
troubles they had getting grown,
the tales of men they told among
themselves as we sat unnoted
at their feet we saw some image
of a past and future self.
The world had loved them even
less than their men but this did
not keep them from scheming on
its favor. It was this that
made them grown and drew from our
unmannerly mouths "Miss"
before their first names.

I call
you Daisy and acknowledge
my place in this line: I am
the women of my childhood
just as I was the women of
my youth, one with these women
of silence who lived on the
cusp of their time and knew it;
who taught what it is to be grown.